TAKING
CHANCES

A GRACE STORY

Book design by Jake Nordby
Illustrations by Jomike Tejido

Published in the United States by Jolly Fish Press, an imprint of North Star Editions, Inc.

First Edition
First Printing, 2018

This is a work of fiction. Names, characters, places, and incidents are either the product of the author's imagination or are used fictitiously, and any resemblance to actual persons living or dead, business establishments, events, or locales is entirely coincidental.

Library of Congress Cataloging-in-Publication Data (pending)
978-1-63163-149-8 (paperback)
978-1-63163-148-1 (hardcover)

Jolly Fish Press
North Star Editions, Inc.
2297 Waters Drive
Mendota Heights, MN 55120
www.jollyfishpress.com

Printed in the United States of America

TAKING
CHANCES

A GRACE STORY

KELSEY ABRAMS

ILLUSTRATED BY JOMIKE TEJIDO

TEXT BY LAURIE J. EDWARDS

JOLLY
FiSH
PRESS

Mendota Heights, Minnesota

Chapter One

Grace Ramirez burst through the door of the family room, where her three sisters were watching TV. It was the second day of summer vacation. "Everyone come out to the barn," she ordered. "I have a surprise."

"Can't it wait?" her oldest sister, Natalie, asked. "We're in the middle of my favorite show, and this is the best part."

"Natalie, you've watched those *Zombie High* DVDs like a gazillion times. You know what happens next," Grace said. "Come on. This'll be the best thing you've ever seen."

Natalie groaned and clicked the channel changer to pause the show. The TV set flickered. "This better be good."

"It will be," Grace promised. She'd been outside kicking her soccer ball and thinking about the circus they'd been to the night before on the county fairgrounds. It had given her a brilliant idea. If that young girl in the circus could do it, so could she. And wouldn't her sisters be stunned to see her do something so daring?

Emily, her twin sister and loyal defender, walked beside her with an excited expression. Natalie appeared a bit bored, and Abby followed at a distance.

When they got to the barn, Grace led her pony, Joker, close to a stack of hay bales. "Here, you hold him, Em, while I get ready."

"Wait a minute, Grace," Natalie said. "You aren't supposed to ride without a helmet."

Grace sighed. The girl in the circus hadn't worn a helmet. She had on a tiara. But when Natalie handed Grace the helmet, she put it on.

Emily took the pony's lead rope and held him in place while Grace scrambled up the bales.

When Grace reached the top, she announced, "And now for the greatest, most daring, death-defying show of all time, Grace Ramirez will balance bareback on Joker."

Emily gasped at the same time as Natalie shouted, "No!"

But Grace ignored them and tried to step onto Joker's back with one foot, ready to raise her other in the air like the bareback rider had done. But before Grace could get her balance, Joker snorted and skittered sideways.

The world whirled around as Grace tumbled through the air and landed with a splat, sprawled across the hay bales, the wind knocked out of her.

"Are you all right?" Emily asked.

Grace's forearms stung, her chest ached, and she'd gotten a mouthful of hay from her face-plant. She tilted her head sideways to spit out the hay but was

too ashamed to lift her eyes and meet her sisters' gazes. Her helmet was askew and covered in hay. At least her long blond hair had flopped over most of her face, preventing them from seeing her flaming cheeks.

Instead of the applause Grace had been hoping for, Abby snorted and Natalie broke into a belly laugh. Even Emily joined in once she saw her sister was okay.

Grace slid down behind the hay bales and slunk out the barn door before any of them could notice the hot, angry tears sliding down her cheeks. Once she was outside, she pounded across the paddock, her sisters' laughter ringing in her ears. When she reached the far end, she climbed the fence, dropped to the other side, and headed for a stand of trees. Just before she reached the trees, she veered to the right. She had a better idea. Miz Ida's garden always calmed her when she was upset.

Behind her, Emily yelled, "Grace, wait!"

Grace glanced over her shoulder. Emily, her blond ponytail bouncing, kicked up dust as she dashed across the dry ground of their ranch. Grace ignored her sister's call and sprinted toward the road. She had to get away. She couldn't face any of them, not even Emily, not now. Maybe not ever.

"Grace Ramirez, don't you dare dash across that road." Emily's words cracked like a whip, and Grace skidded to a stop.

A few seconds later, a red pickup raced past at about eighty miles an hour. Grace drew in a shuddery breath. She could have been flattened.

Emily caught up to her. Emily bent over, hands on her knees, her chest heaving in and out with quick, harsh pants. "That . . . was . . . close."

Grace snorted. "You sound like a dog. Better be careful, or I'll ask Abby what breed you are." Their sister Abby loved dogs and had memorized every dog fact possible, turning herself into a walking encyclopedia.

Instead of being upset, Emily flashed her a good-natured smile. "I'm winded because I don't play soccer like you do."

"Yeah, you sit around all day drawing or reading books." The only outdoor activity Emily enjoyed was riding horses. Most of the time, Grace had to coax her sister to come outside and play. If only she hadn't convinced all her sisters to come out to the barn to see her trick. Her cheeks heated again even thinking about it. She'd made such a fool of herself.

She swiped her fists across her cheeks to wipe away the wetness. She didn't mind if Emily saw her cry because Emily was different. No matter what Grace did, her sister loved her and forgave her. But her older sisters were different, Natalie especially. "I just wanted to show Natalie I could do something she couldn't do," Grace burst out. "Whatever I try, she can do it better."

"That's only because she's older. When you're twelve like Natalie, you'll be able to do everything she does now. You might even be able to do it better."

"By then, she'll be fifteen, so she'll still be doing everything better than me. Way better. I'll never catch up."

Emily smiled. "Why do you have to catch up? Why don't you let Natalie be the best Natalie she can be, and you be the best Grace you can be?"

In her heart, Grace knew Emily was right, but that didn't take away the sting of everyone's laughter. Life was so easy for Emily. She accepted people the way they were. She always thought before she acted and never made embarrassing mistakes. "But everyone laughed at me."

"Come on, Grace. If Natalie tried to stand on her horse and fell off onto a pile of hay, wouldn't you laugh?"

"I guess," Grace said sullenly. "But Natalie wouldn't do something like that."

"Exactly. Maybe if you didn't try to show off . . ." Emily suggested, her tone gentle.

"I thought it would be easy. The girl at the circus did it."

Emily leaned over and picked a few bits of loose hay from Grace's hair. "I'm sure she practiced for a long time before she tried. How long did you practice?"

Grace hung her head and shuffled her feet in the

dirt. "I didn't practice at all," she admitted. "I just had the idea and tried it."

"Those horses are specially trained too. Of all our horses, Joker is one of the most skittish. You might have been badly hurt if you hadn't landed on hay. What were you thinking?"

"I-I wasn't," Grace stammered. At least not about the dangers. All she'd been thinking about was hearing everyone *ooh* and *aah*.

Her sister didn't say a word, only looked at Grace.

"I know, I know." Grace waved a hand in the air. "Mom always tells me not to rush headlong into things, but it's hard when I get all these great ideas and I want to do them right away."

"I understand," Emily assured her. "You're lucky to have so many fun ideas, and you're brave enough to try them. I wish I could be more like that."

"You do? But I'm always getting into trouble."

"Not always. Sometimes you come up with the coolest plans."

"I wish I had today," Grace said. "Then everyone wouldn't be laughing at me." That reminded her of her destination—Miz Ida's garden. Grace stomped along beside the split-rail fence separating their ranch from the road, heading in the direction of her friend's house.

"Are we crossing here?" Emily asked when they'd

walked the length of their yard and were directly across from Miz Ida's ranch.

"Um, Em?" Grace hesitated to hurt her sister's feelings after she'd been so kind and understanding. "It's not that I don't want your company, it's just that . . ."

Emily held up a hand. "I know you like visiting Miz Ida alone. I want to be sure you get across the street safely."

Grace was stung by her sister's words. "I'm not a baby."

"Of course not. We're the same age, remember?" Emily teased. "But you almost . . ."

Yeah, I almost got hit by a truck, so now she thinks she needs to help me cross the street. And back at the house, Natalie and Abby are probably still giggling about my belly flop. And everyone will be talking about it at dinner tonight.

Grace's face heated and her eyes burned.

Some days the ache for her birth mom was worse than others. Emily stayed so quiet, she blended into the background and fit in anywhere they went. People automatically liked her. But Grace always, *always* did things that made her stand out in a crowd and in her family. But not in a good way. At least it seemed that way.

Chapter Two

Instead of heading for Miz Ida's front door, Grace walked up the long driveway and veered toward the side yard of the one-story house, where a tall wooden fence enclosed Miz Ida's garden. Most mornings that's where Grace found her elderly friend. Miz Ida had told her she was welcome in the garden any time, and Grace visited as often as she could after the never-ending chores of caring for the animals at Second Chance Ranch.

As soon as Grace unlatched the gate, her spirits lifted. The heady aroma of roses greeted her. She cupped one of her favorites, the Secret, and tipped her head to inhale the sweetness of the cream rose. She loved the pink tint on the outer edges and the gold hidden near the base of each petal that only showed when the rose opened. She guessed that secret gold had given the flower its name, but she'd have to ask Miz Ida. Breathing in the scent always calmed Grace, and a sense of peace washed over her.

Miz Ida knelt on the cushion she used for her arthritis, pulling up weeds in the vegetable garden. Near the back fence, the tomato plants stood tall and green against the six-foot stakes, and plump red tomatoes hung heavy on the branches. Grace had helped to place rocks by each tomato plant to save the plants from drought during the dry summer weather. The bean plants had wound their way up the poles, and green beans dangled among the leaves. Everywhere she looked, plants were healthy and blooming, including Miz Ida's roses.

Grace waved to get her attention, and Miz Ida's wrinkled face lit up. "I was hoping you'd show up today. I could use some help." She pointed to the bucket on the steps. "Could you bring those scraps over and put them on the compost pile?"

"Sure." Grace picked up the bucket from Miz Ida's concrete steps. The bucket held slimy lettuce leaves and decaying vegetable peels. This part of gardening turned her stomach, but Miz Ida assured her plants loved the icky, smelly mess. Grace wanted to hold her nose when she dumped the scraps onto the compost pile, but she'd been trying to prove to Miz Ida that she was a good gardener.

"Did you remember to add some brown?" Miz Ida asked after Grace rinsed out the bucket and set it on the back stoop.

"Oops, I forgot." Grace went back and sprinkled some dry leaves and straw over the top.

Miz Ida had taught her that food scraps were called *green*, and the grasses, leaves, straw, and twigs were *brown*. A good compost pile needed layers of both. She'd explained about brown being rich in carbon and green adding nitrogen, but Grace hadn't listened much after that. All she remembered was that the stuff in the bottom of the compost bin fed the plants.

When Grace rejoined her, Miz Ida smiled. "How are you this fine day?"

Although the roses had calmed her, Miz Ida's question reminded Grace of the reason she'd fled to the garden. "Mad . . . sad . . . embarrassed." The words flowed out of her mouth, and when Miz Ida raised her eyebrows to encourage Grace to continue,

Grace wished she could stuff those words back inside. But now that she'd let them out, Miz Ida wouldn't let it rest until she found out the whole story, so Grace recounted the incident in the barn and the tinkling laughter that followed.

After she finished, Grace added, "Maybe they didn't mean to hurt my feelings, but they did. And they do it all the time."

"Really?" Miz Ida tipped her head to the side like the little chickadees perched on the fence. "All the time?"

"Well, not all the time," Grace admitted. "Only some of the time."

"And they're mean on purpose?"

Grace squirmed. Usually Miz Ida let her talk without judging her or criticizing her, but today she seemed to be contradicting everything Grace said. Grace wanted to stamp her foot. First Emily, now Miz Ida. Why did everyone have to be so logical and so right? Why couldn't they just agree with her?

"Okay, so they're not mean on purpose," Grace said grudgingly. "But they didn't have to laugh at me."

"That hurt your feelings," Miz Ida said.

Grace nodded. "It hurt a lot. Nobody else in the family makes all the embarrassing mistakes I do. Nobody else gets in trouble as much as I do."

Miz Ida slid her cushion a little farther down the

row and pulled several weeds before she spoke. "Why do you suppose that is, Grace?"

"I don't know." Grace scuffed her toe on the ground in front of her. Actually, she had an idea, but she didn't want to admit it.

Miz Ida motioned to the row beside her. "I'd love some help with the weeds, if you don't mind."

Grace grabbed a trowel from Miz Ida's bucket and squatted down to pull weeds. *Yank, toss. Yank, toss. Yank, toss.* The rhythmic motion soothed her. Partway down the row, she started giggling. "Remember the first time I helped you in the garden?"

"Indeed I do." Miz Ida laughed. "You were right eager to help, but—"

"I ripped up the plants instead of the weeds," Grace finished her sentence.

"You've learned a lot since then," Miz Ida said, nodding. "Gardening takes patience."

And patience was something Grace didn't have. She always rushed headlong into everything, which landed her in trouble. She heaved a huge sigh as she twisted her trowel under a stubborn weed and dug it out.

"You sound like you have the weight of the world on your shoulders today."

No, only the weight of her foolish ideas. "I wish I could be patient and think before I do things," Grace said. If she had, she wouldn't be headed back to the laughter of her family.

"You learned to be patient when you're gardening," Miz Ida pointed out.

Grace leaned back on her heels. That was true. Maybe that's why she loved coming to Miz Ida's. Digging in the dirt took time, and it slowed the frantic whirling in Grace's brain.

Miz Ida pressed her hands against the small of her back and stretched. Then she groaned. She sounded like she was in pain.

The sound alarmed Grace. "Are you all right?"

"Fine, fine." Miz Ida's voice was brisk. "These old bones aren't what they used to be." She struggled to her feet. "I'm heading inside for some sweet tea. Would you like something to drink?"

"I only finished one row," Grace said, "and the tomatoes, beans, and peppers still need to be picked."

"Cucumbers, too, but you can finish that later." Miz Ida tottered toward the back steps. "I have something I want to discuss with you."

Grace tossed down her trowel and jumped to her feet. Miz Ida's words had sounded almost ominous.

Chapter Three

Grace rushed after Miz Ida. "Is everything all right?" she demanded.

Miz Ida clung to the metal railing and hauled herself up one step at a time. Stopping for breath on the back porch, she said, "That's what I wanted to talk to you about."

"You're not sick or anything, are you?" Grace bounded past her. She opened the screen door for Miz Ida, then waited while she fumbled with the doorknob on the back door.

"Oh no, dear." Miz Ida headed for the refrigerator. "I'm just getting old and tired."

"You're not old," Grace protested. She headed for the cupboard where Miz Ida kept her glasses and took down two.

"Let's get our drinks and sit in the living room." Miz Ida opened her old-fashioned white refrigerator and took out a pitcher of sweet tea.

Grace loved Miz Ida's kitchen. Unlike her own house with its rustic wooden Southwestern furniture and clean lines, Miz Ida's house was stuffed full of antiques and dainty, ruffled, puffy furniture. Her cluttered kitchen counters and her refrigerator covered with magnets, notes, photos, and brochures were so different from Grace's house with its *everything-in-its-proper-place* countertops. Only abuela's pottery decorated the counters, and Emily's drawings hung neatly on the refrigerator.

"Lemonade for you?" Miz Ida asked.

Grace nodded. Her mom made unsweetened iced tea and stirred in a little sugar, but Miz Ida grew up in the South, and her tea was so sweet it made Grace's teeth hurt. She preferred Miz Ida's lemonade, which was tart enough to make her mouth pucker. Grace jiggled from one foot to the other while Miz Ida snipped two sprigs of mint from a windowsill jammed with potted herbs and dropped one sprig in each glass. She wanted to hear what Miz Ida had to say.

Miz Ida puttered around her kitchen, plucking dead leaves from the herbs, placing a quilted cover over her toaster, putting away the dishes she had left to dry on the counter. She hummed to herself and kept doing small chores until Grace was ready to burst. In the garden, she'd decided she wanted to learn to be patient, but she'd already changed her mind. Waiting made her too antsy. She wanted to be doing something, anything. If Miz Ida had news, Grace wanted to hear it now, right this minute.

She couldn't stand it any longer. "Miz Ida, what did you want to talk about?"

"Hmm?" Miz Ida turned toward her. "Oh, Grace

dear, you were so quiet, I almost forgot you were here. Let's go have our talk."

"I'll carry the glasses." Grace grabbed for the drinks, and they almost sloshed over the sides. She forced herself to slow down and balance while she followed Miz Ida into the other room. She set the sweet tea on the coaster beside Miz Ida's chair.

Miz Ida lowered herself into the hard-backed chair she preferred because she said it was easier for her to get her old bones out of. Grace sat on the couch across from her and took a sip of lemonade.

"Ouch!" Grace jumped and almost spilled her glass. She set the lemonade on a coaster and leaned down to rub her ankle. Then she dropped to her knees and lifted the couch skirt. "Come on out from under there, Chances." She reached for the snowy white Persian and eased her out from under the sofa. "You scratched my ankle, you sneaky thing."

Chances had earned her name as a kitten when Miz Ida took two chances: one on buying a purebred cat to ease her loneliness after her husband died, and the other on picking the scrawniest cat in the litter. Miz Ida said they'd been lucky chances because her kitten turned into a good companion and a championship cat.

Chances was an unusual white Persian with two different colored eyes. One eye was a beautiful blue, almost turquoise, one of Emily's favorite colors. The

other eye was amber. In sunlight it appeared almost yellow, but in the shadows, it looked closer to brown. Her eyes gave Chances a mysterious and exotic look.

Grace settled back onto the couch and ran her hands along the cat's silky fur until Chances kneaded a spot in her lap and curled up. Loud purring rumbled through Chances's fluffy body. Grace loved Miz Ida's cat almost as much as she loved Miz Ida.

"Have you brushed Chances yet today?" Grace asked. Miz Ida had explained that championship cats needed to be brushed daily to remove tangles and keep their skin healthy. Brushing also removed loose hair so Chances wouldn't lick and swallow her fur and cough up hairballs.

"Not yet. Would you like to do it?" Miz Ida replied.

"Yes." Grace almost jumped to her feet but remembered Chances just in time. She slid the cat onto the sofa cushion beside her and ran for the comb and brush and mat. Miz Ida always set Chances on a special mat to catch any hair that drifted down.

When she returned to the living room, Grace put Chances on the mat. Beginning at Chance's head, she combed backwards with the wide-toothed metal comb. When she reached Chance's sides, she lifted the fur and combed down a little at a time.

Miz Ida smiled. "You do such a good job with that."

"I remember what you taught me." Grace switched

to the brush, going from Chance's tail to head and then brushing upward on each side.

"You do a good a job in the garden too. That makes me feel confident about asking you to watch Chances and care for the garden while I'm gone," Miz Ida said.

"You're going away?" Grace couldn't help being surprised. Miz Ida had never gone anywhere except to the grocery store, doctor's office, and church since Grace had moved to the ranch three years ago.

Miz Ida nodded. "I admit I'm a little nervous about going away, but I know I can count on you to take care of everything here while I'm gone." She looked at Grace with a question in her eyes. "You will do that for me, won't you?"

"Of course," Grace answered without hesitation. She'd be happy to do it.

"Good, good." Miz Ida reached into the drawer of the table beside her and pulled out a tablet of paper and a pen. "Let me make a list of chores for you."

After her pen stopped scratching on the paper, she tore off the sheet and handed it to Grace, who struggled to read the spidery handwriting:

Feed Chances
Give Chances fresh water
Clean litter box
Brush the cat
Water kitchen herbs

Weed garden
Tend compost pile
Water plants in morning
Pick ripe vegetables
Pick beetles off roses

Grace nodded. She'd done all these jobs alongside Miz Ida for the past few years. She should be able to manage them alone. "But where will you be?"

"My son wants me to come for a visit. He's worried about me living alone. He suggested I might want to move to Arizona and stay with them."

Grace had met Miz Ida's son, Roger, last summer when he and his family came for a visit. He and his wife seemed very nice, and his children, who were teenagers, even let Grace play video games with them. But she didn't want Miz Ida to move so far away.

"You're not going to move, are you?"

Miz Ida leaned back in her chair and closed her eyes. "I don't want to make a hasty decision, but sometimes taking chances is a good thing."

"Like you did with Chances." Keeping one hand on the cat, Grace leaned over and lifted her glass of lemonade.

"Exactly." Miz Ida set her sweet tea glass on a coaster and fiddled with a small wooden carving of a bird. "I took a chance on moving here to Texas with my husband when he retired. I was nervous about it because I'd never lived anywhere but Georgia."

"But if you hadn't moved, I never would have met you," Grace said.

Grace tried to imagine what her life would have been like without Miz Ida, who had provided comfort and a listening ear when Grace and Emily arrived at the ranch several days after their mom's death. Grace had not only agonized over losing her mom, but she'd also struggled to adapt to the ranch after growing up in the city. She couldn't have adjusted here without Miz Ida's help.

Chances batted Grace's arm to remind her she'd stopped brushing her while she was lost in thought. "Sorry, Chances." Grace scratched a spot behind Chances's ear until the cat stretched and purred. "You're done with your brushing for the day." Grace picked up the mat, walked to the back porch to shake the fur outside for the birds to use for nests, and put away the grooming tools. Then she settled Chances back in her lap.

Miz Ida had a faraway look in her eyes, and her face had settled into lines of sadness. She sometimes did that when she thought about her husband.

Grace wanted to cheer her up. "I'd never been friends with—" Grace almost said *an old lady,* but quickly changed her mind. ". . . err, someone who wasn't my age, but I'm glad I took a chance," she finished.

Natalie and Abby had stayed away from Miz Ida.

She always seemed to be busy in her garden and never waved or spoke when she saw the girls. But one day, Grace accidentally kicked her soccer ball into Miz Ida's yard. She took a chance and talked to the elderly lady. That's when she learned Miz Ida was lonesome, but with her failing eyesight and hearing, she couldn't see or hear anyone unless they were close. She'd recently lost her husband, so she understood Grace's grieving for her mom.

"I wouldn't have made it here at the ranch without you," Grace said.

"I'm glad I could help." Miz Ida's managed a wobbly smile. "Until you showed up, Grace dear, I was a very lonely woman. I count you among my greatest blessings."

Grace's eyes stung. People had called her many things during her life, but no one had ever called her a blessing.

As if sensing her owner's distress, Chances hopped off Grace's lap, stretched, and with her tail swishing, strutted over to rub against Miz Ida's legs. Miz Ida bent to run her fingers through the Persian's fur. "Yes, Chances, you helped too.

"Taking chances can be a good thing," Miz Ida said, "but I don't want to rush into things. My mama always warned me to think before I acted or I'd end up in trouble."

"I know what you mean." Grace had found that out the hard way.

"Unfortunately, I didn't heed my mama's advice when I was young, but now that I'm older, I realize how important it is to consider all my options before I make a decision. I still make room for taking chances, but not foolish ones."

Grace hung her head. "Like my bareback riding this morning."

"You learned a valuable lesson, though." Miz Ida stood. "Are you done with your lemonade?" She reached for Grace's empty glass. "I'll get these washed and put away."

"I can do it." Grace jumped up and nearly knocked the glass from Miz Ida's hands.

"Thanks for the offer, but I think it'd be better if I did it myself." Miz Ida's kind smile took some of the sting out of her words.

Grace trailed her to the kitchen. "Should I finish the weed—" She stopped short when she caught sight of Miz Ida's kitchen clock. "Oh, I'm late for my afternoon chores!"

Before Grace could rush out the door, Miz Ida stopped her. "Oh, silly me. I forgot to tell you how much I'd be paying you." She named a sum that made Grace's jaw drop.

"I couldn't take that much money from you," Grace said.

"You'll earn it, believe me. And if you feel it's still too much after the two weeks are up, you can give the rest to your parents for the ranch."

"Thank you," Grace called as she ran across the lawn. Remembering the speeding truck that morning, she checked both ways before crossing the road. She sneaked into the barn and began cleaning water buckets.

"Emily," Natalie yelled across the yard, "tell Grace it's time to get out to the barn."

"I'm right here," Grace said behind her.

Natalie jumped, making Grace feel a little guilty.

Her sister's eyebrows shot up. "You're already cleaning without being told?" Natalie asked. "Good for you."

While Grace did her chores, she concentrated on every detail of her conversation with Miz Ida. Her favorite part was being called a blessing, but she also mentally reviewed the long list of chores Miz Ida had given her.

Once again she'd jumped into things without thinking. Taking care of the garden all by herself and remembering to feed Chances and keeping an eye on the empty house now seemed like a lot of responsibility. If she'd thought about all the work first, she might not have agreed. But maybe this was a chance worth taking. She'd do anything for Miz Ida, anything at all.

Chapter Four

Grace dawdled on her chores, wishing she wouldn't ever have to go in for dinner. Somebody was bound to tell her parents about this morning's failed circus act. If her stomach hadn't been growling, she might have skipped dinner and hidden out in her room, but all she'd had that afternoon was a glass of lemonade.

Just before she finished her chores, a horse trailer rattled down the dirt driveway that led to the barn, and a stranger hopped out. Natalie started for the driveway, but Grace waved her off. "I'll get it," she said. Grace strode over to greet the man. Her dad hadn't mentioned they were getting another horse, but what a nice a surprise.

The man tipped his hat. "This here Second Chance Ranch?" When Grace nodded, he heaved a sigh. "Good. I understand you rescue animals."

"Yes, we do." So maybe no one knew about this horse's arrival.

"All kinds of animals?"

"Of course," Grace said proudly, pointing to Portobello, their potbellied pig, snuffling in the yard nearby. They'd be losing him soon because a lady had fallen in love with his picture on the ranch's website.

She'd be picking him up this weekend. Grace was going to miss Portobello; she'd grown attached to him.

"Good, good," the man mumbled. "Should I unload here?"

"Why don't you back down closer to the barn while I get my sister," Grace said. "She's the horse expert."

The man rubbed the back of his neck. "Well, the thing is . . . See, I don't have a horse in there. I just didn't know how else to transport it."

Grace followed him to the back of the trailer. He swung open the doors and lowered the ramp. The huge brown bird inside must have lowered its long neck to fit into the horse trailer. As soon as the doors opened, it ducked and poked its small head outside. With round amber eyes and sparse, spiky gray feathers sticking out around its head, the bird looked surprised as the man led it down the ramp.

Grace's mouth hung open as the bird stretched to its full height. It had to be taller than her dad.

"Um, what is it?" She was uncertain whether they accepted birds like this, but she'd already bragged that they took all animals.

"An emu."

Grace had heard of them, but she'd never seen one up close. "They don't fly, do they?"

"Nope," the man said. "Sad to say, it won't be flying away. I found this poor guy wandering around near the highway. Somebody must have abandoned it."

Grace couldn't imagine abandoning a bird this huge. "Is it sick or something? Is that why they didn't want it?" she wondered aloud. If the bird was ill, her mom wouldn't let it near the other animals. As a vet, Mrs. Ramirez took plenty of precautions to be sure all the animals stayed healthy. But she wasn't home from work yet to look at it.

"It's sad, but a lot of people abandon them. Emu chicks are so tiny and cute with their striped, feathery ducklike bodies and tiny, pointy beaks. Many people snap them up, never considering where they'll keep the full-grown bird."

A car pulled into the driveway, and Grace waved to Mrs. Ramirez. "Here's my mother now. She's a vet, so she'll check out the emu."

The man nodded and closed up his trailer. He was making his way back to Grace when Mrs. Ramirez headed toward them. Her eyes opened wide when she spotted the emu.

"Grace, what in the world?" Mrs. Ramirez looked dumbfounded.

"It's an emu," Grace said, sheepishly.

"I can see that, but what—" Before Mrs. Ramirez could finish her sentence, the man stepped toward her and tipped his hat.

"I can explain, ma'am," he said. "I found this bird wandering over by the highway. I was afraid it would get hit, so I brought it here." He gave her a winning smile. "Your daughter here assured me you take abandoned animals."

"We do, but we've never had an emu before," Mrs. Ramirez said. Then she sighed and turned to Grace. "Well, I guess since you accepted the bird, you'll need to research how to care for and feed emus."

Grace gulped. The huge bird frightened her. She didn't want to be responsible for caring for it.

With a quick "thank you," the man got back in his truck and drove off, leaving a trail of dust in his wake and Grace with a hundred-pound pet.

"Put him in the back pen until I can check him over," Mrs. Ramirez said. "After dinner we'll have to figure out what to feed him. For now, give him some water to drink." She tucked a loose piece of hair back into her bun. "Poor thing is probably thirsty."

Poor thing? This giant bird towered over her, and Mrs. Ramirez was talking about it as if it were a chick.

The man had left a leash dangling around the emu's neck, so after two tries to grab it—Grace stopped both times when the emu turned its beady eyes on her—she finally picked it up, accidentally brushing the bird's feathers with the back of her hand. They were amazingly soft. She'd expected the huge bird to have rough, coarse feathers.

Holding the very end of the leash and staying as far away from the huge bird as she could, Grace led

it to the pen Mrs. Ramirez had suggested, hoping it wouldn't lean over and peck her. Its long neck could easily stretch the length of the leash.

When Grace returned with a water pail, Emily was sitting on a nearby split-rail fence, sketching the emu. Grace set the water pail inside the pen and skittered to slam the door shut while the emu was facing the other direction. She latched the pen and stepped far enough away to be out of pecking distance.

She had no idea if emus liked to peck people, and she didn't want to find out.

Emily jumped down from the fence and set her sketchbook on top of the backpack she used for art supplies. "You're not leaving that leash around the poor bird's neck, are you? It might choke."

Grace ran a hand across her forehead. They never left dangling ropes or leashes that could catch on things and hurt the animals. But just looking at the towering emu, Grace froze. She couldn't, wouldn't go into that small pen with a possible killer bird.

"I can't, Em." Grace said. "What if it bites me?"

"Oh, Grace, animals usually treat you the way you treat them. If you're kind, they'll be kind." Emily unlatched the gate and marched into the pen. After closing it behind her, she stood still and made eye contact with the emu. The two of them stared at each other, and Emily gave it a gentle smile. She took a few steps toward the emu and watched it closely. The emu took several steps toward Emily.

"Would you like me to take off that collar for you?" Emily's tone was soft and soothing.

The emu moved closer, then so did Emily. They took turns, one moving and then the other.

Although she was frightened for her sister, Grace also was fascinated. It was almost like the two of them were dancing. She held her breath as Emily took the final two steps and reached for the collar. The bird lifted its neck, and Grace sucked in a breath. But the emu only swayed toward Emily so she could reach around and unhook the collar.

Her sister had her arms around the emu's neck, and she leaned her face against its feathery side as she removed the collar, all the while murmuring words Grace couldn't hear. After the leash was off, Emily stroked the emu for a while. Then she backed up and waved goodbye.

Did emus smile? Grace could have sworn this one did. But when Emily let herself out the gate, the emu's eyes appeared sad. So did Emily.

"I'm sorry you have to be in such a small pen, but after Mom examines you, maybe you'll be allowed to go free," Emily said to the bird.

"You talk to the animals as if they can understand you," Grace said to her sister.

Emily glanced at her in surprise. "Of course they can, and they always answer."

"Oh." Grace wasn't sure she'd ever had a conversation with an animal who answered her back. "They answer in words?"

"No, you don't need words, although I use them sometimes," Emily said. "But it's more like a feeling, a sense. I don't know how to explain it, but you just know deep inside what they're saying." Emily walked over, picked up her sketchbook, and climbed back on the fence rail.

Grace trailed after her. "I've never heard them say anything."

"I think you have to be very, very quiet to hear it." Emily opened to a fresh page in her sketchbook. "Now that I've been close to the emu and actually touched it, I can draw it a little better."

Grace knew once Emily was absorbed in her drawing, the world around her sister would disappear. Emily went into this secret world and shut Grace out. Sometimes she stayed there for hours, leaving Grace lonely, even when they were in the same room. Maybe that also was the world where she heard animals speak.

Chapter Five

Grace washed up for dinner and headed to the table with a huge knot of dread twisting in her stomach. Even though it was pizza night, her favorite night of the week, she took only one slice, ducked her head, and ate it without making eye contact.

The tangled knots in her stomach pulled even tighter when Mr. Ramirez started the usual conversation. "So who wants to be first to tell us about their day?"

Most nights Grace was bursting with news she couldn't wait to share. She hated sitting quietly and listening until it was her turn. Often the family let her begin because until it was her turn, she wriggled in her chair so much she shook the table. Tonight, though, she cringed. Who would be the first to tell on her daring attempt in the barn this morning?

One by one, they took their turns. Natalie had updated the website with pictures and descriptions of their newest animals. "I even managed to get the emu posted before dinner, and we got several donations today," she said.

Mrs. Ramirez set a piece of spinach and sun-dried tomato pizza on her plate. "That's great, Natalie. We really appreciate you doing that," she said, and then sighed. "I had a tough day today. Tina tipped her coffee mug over, and it fell into an open file drawer. Most of the records in the drawer were soaked. We spread them out all over to dry, but many are stained and some are illegible."

Natalie waved a hand in front of her mouth to indicate she wanted to talk but had to finish chewing first. Then she said, "Mom, I keep telling you, you need to update the computer files. Nobody uses paper files anymore."

Mrs. Ramirez sighed again. "I'm so busy taking care of animals, I don't have time, and Tina's just as busy handling patient registration, scheduling, billing, and helping me when needed."

"Then I'll come in for a few hours a day and help set it up," Natalie said. "Darcy is visiting her dad in Hawai'i for the summer anyway, so I have time. You can't live in the Dark Ages forever, mom!" She giggled.

Wow! Natalie's generosity impressed Grace. *Natalie would give up watching* Zombie High *and training horses to help Mom?* Plus, Natalie hadn't said a word about Grace's fiasco that morning.

Abby gushed about the puppies that still had a few weeks at the ranch before they went to their new homes. "Oh, and I researched emus and learned a lot. Their legs are extremely powerful, so they kick hard if they're upset."

If this had been an ordinary night, Grace would

have interrupted Abby to tell about Emily's connection with the emu when she removed the leash. Tonight, though, she stayed silent.

Abby shared a few more emu facts and then selected a slice of cheese pizza. Grace released a pent-up breath. Two down, and no mention of her bareback-riding attempt. She was pretty sure Emily wouldn't betray her.

Emily reached for the sketchbook beside her plate and flipped it open. "I sketched the emu this afternoon. I've never seen a live one before." She held up two pages filled with the emu in different positions—running, stretching, bending down. "Tomorrow after the trail ride, I'll enlarge one and paint it."

The trail ride. Grace had forgotten all about their plans to pack a picnic lunch and go on a long trail ride. She couldn't go along. She'd promised Miz Ida she'd come over for training. Once again, she almost broke into the conversation to say that, but she caught herself in time. This keeping silent was horrid. But saying something would be worse.

"Grace, you're awfully quiet tonight," Mr. Ramirez said. "What did you do today?"

If nobody else had mentioned her disaster, Grace wouldn't either. She raised her chin and said, "I went to visit Miz Ida and helped her in the garden. She's going to Arizona to visit her son for two weeks, and she wants me to take care of Chances and weed the garden and pick the vegetables and keep an eye on her house while she's away." She didn't pause for breath. She was afraid that if she did, one of her sisters might tattle about the morning.

Mr. Ramirez looked thoughtful. "That seems like an awful lot of responsibility. Are you sure you're going to be able to handle all that and keep up with your chores around here? Also, I heard you're in charge of learning about and handling the emu."

"I'll take care of handling the emu," Emily volunteered. "I'd like to spend more time around him so I can photograph and paint him."

"I can give you all the information I looked up about emus," Abby said. She pulled the cheese off her pizza to eat separately. She didn't like her food mixed together.

Natalie took an extra helping of salad. "I could take care of Grace's horse duties in the morning."

"That's thoughtful of you, Natalie, but you already offered to help me at the office," Mrs. Ramirez said. "You need to have some fun on your summer vacation."

"I don't mind." Natalie speared a cherry tomato with her fork. "Taking care of horses is fun for me, and it'll only be two weeks."

"I'm proud of all of you for being so willing to help out." Mr. Ramirez smiled at the three girls and then turned to Grace.

Grace sat in stunned silence. The sisters who only this morning had been laughing at her now were going out of their way to help her. "Thank you," was all she could manage to say.

Later that night, as Grace and Mrs. Ramirez were doing the dishes together, the phone rang. After a tense conversation, Mrs. Ramirez tossed the dish-towel to her husband in the family room. "I have to head out to the Hernandez farm. One of their horses is hurt."

Mr. Ramirez sighed. "I wish you'd take on a partner. You work much too hard." He kissed her good-bye. "Drive carefully and call if you need anything," he called after her.

He came into the kitchen with the dish towel slung over his shoulder. "It's you and me, kiddo," he said to Grace. "What's left to dry?"

Grace handed him one of abuela's pottery plates and swished her hands around in the sudsy water for the next one.

"So tell me more about Miz Ida's job opportunity," Mr. Ramirez said as he dried the plate.

After bottling up her comments for most of the day, it was a relief to talk nonstop. Grace told him about all the things they'd done and talked about, except Miz Ida saying Grace was a blessing. She kept that to herself.

"Anyway, even though she sometimes takes chances, she says she doesn't want to jump into moving to Arizona without thinking." Grace handed Mr. Ramirez some silverware.

"That sounds like wise advice," he said.

Grace couldn't tell if he meant in general or if he was directing that comment to her because she rushed headlong into things. She wasn't sure, so she kept silent.

Mr. Ramirez slid open the drawer near him and placed the silverware in the dividers. "I'm sure you'll do a fine job."

"Oh, and I forgot to tell you how much she's going to pay me!"

Mr. Ramirez whistled when she told him the amount. "She must think very highly of your work to offer that much money."

"I told her I wasn't worth that much, and she said I could donate the extra to the ranch. But I think I'd rather keep it all for myself," Grace said.

Mr. Ramirez laughed. "I hope you'll consider some other options. Like maybe putting some of it in the bank." He dried the last of the silverware and put it away while Grace drained and rinsed the sink. "Time for bed, kiddo. I'll be up soon to tuck you in."

"It's still light out, and it's summer." Grace always tried to wheedle a little extra time before bed.

"Tell that to the animals in the morning when you oversleep," Mr. Ramirez said over his shoulder as he went to join Natalie in the family room. "Call me when you and Emily are done with your showers and are in bed."

Grace wanted to drag out her bedtime, but she had Miz Ida's to look forward to tomorrow morning. She let Emily take a shower first, then she took her turn and called for Mr. Ramirez as soon as they were both in bed. As usual, Emily was absorbed in a book.

Mr. Ramirez came bounding up the stairs. As hard as it was to believe now, when she and Emily first arrived at the ranch, Grace had been scared of him. Her birth mom had been a single mother, so Grace wasn't used to sharing a house with a tall man who had a deep voice.

The first night he and Mrs. Ramirez came into the bedroom to hug them good night, Grace had been so frightened she'd shivered and backed away. His arms, strong and muscular from all the work around the ranch, looked like they might crush her. Yet she'd been surprised by his softness. He had gently picked her up, tucked her in bed, and read her and Emily a story. She loved how he changed his voice to high and squeaky for a mouse and then low and growly for a bear. Even after the girls claimed to be too old for bedtime stories, he still sometimes came in and read a chapter book with them. Now Grace was grateful to have a dad, especially one who cared about them so much. And she looked forward to nightly hugs from Mr. and Mrs. Ramirez.

After he hugged Emily, Mr. Ramirez sat on the foot of Grace's bed. "There's something I need to talk to you about." His usual smile turned into a serious expression. "I understand you did something danger-ous in the barn this morning."

Grace's fists clenched at her sides. "Who told you that?"

"It doesn't matter. What matters is—"

"Yes, it does matter!" Grace bolted to an upright position. "If someone tattled on me, I should know who."

The frown lines on Mr. Ramirez's brow grew deeper. "Grace, the point is about your safety and that of the horses."

"The horses? It was Natalie, wasn't it?" She could tell by Mr. Ramirez's expression she was right. Grace bounced up and down on the bed. She was so upset, she could hardly control herself.

"Calm down, Grace." Mr. Ramirez set his hands

on her shoulders. "Do you want to tell me your side of the story?"

Grace slumped back against her pillow and hung her head. "No," she said in a small voice. She wished she could go back and erase the memory in her own head and the ones in her sisters' minds.

"All right, then. I'd like you to listen to me," Mr. Ramirez said patiently. "I'm sure you've already discovered some of the dangers today, but you could have been badly hurt if Joker had bucked, and it's possible you could have hurt him."

Grace couldn't look Mr. Ramirez in the eye, so she pleated the edge of the sheet between her fingers. "I'm sorry," she said.

"I know you are, and I'm sure now that you've had a chance to reflect on it, you understand why it wasn't a wise choice." Mr. Ramirez reached out and set his strong, tanned hand over her fingers. "Mom isn't here to talk it over, but I've decided to take away your riding privileges for two weeks. That means no trail ride tomorrow."

Grace couldn't go on the trail ride tomorrow anyway, but she kept that to herself. Actually, she'd be working at Miz Ida's for the next two weeks, so it wouldn't be so bad. After this morning, she didn't really want to ride a horse, even if she'd miss her special times with her pony. "Who's going to exercise Joker?" she asked.

"Natalie or I can do it," Emily said from the bed next to her.

"Thank you, Emily," Mr. Ramirez said. He leaned over and kissed Grace's forehead. "I hope you realize we're not punishing you to be mean. We're doing it because we love you. We care about you and want to keep you safe."

"I know," Grace mumbled. She couldn't believe him, at least not right now. Even though they'd had this same conversation before, this was the first time she'd ever lost riding privileges, and that hurt.

When Mr. Ramirez left, Grace lay still for a long while, staring at the ceiling. Would there ever come a day when she didn't get into trouble?

In the bed nearby, Emily's breathing fell into a natural, even rhythm.

As the darkness closed around her, Grace whispered to herself, "Miz Ida thinks I'm a blessing."

Too bad no one else does.

Chapter Six

Excited to get started at Miz Ida's, Grace rose early the next morning. She hurried through her chores, doing as little as possible, and rushed from the barn.

"Come back here!" Natalie called after her. She stood, legs apart and hands on her hips, frowning. "I agreed to help with your share of the morning horse duties while you're working for Miz Ida, but that doesn't mean I'm starting today."

"I already did my jobs," Grace mumbled.

Natalie's voice softened. "I know you're eager to get to Miz Ida's, but our horses deserve proper care. You need to get back in there and do it right this time."

Grace knew she was right, but she stomped back to the stalls just to prove a point.

After she finished with the horses and Natalie had inspected her work, Grace scooted from the barn. In her rush, she almost mowed down Emily, who was carrying a new bag of feed for the rabbits.

"Someone didn't refill the feed bin," Emily said. Emily hadn't said anybody's name, but they both knew whose job it was: Grace's.

"Sorry," Grace said. "I was in a hurry and forgot."

"Did you feed the rabbits their salads?" Emily asked.

Grace couldn't look Emily in the eye. "No," she said sheepishly. She'd only changed their water and given them fresh Timothy hay.

Emily didn't scold her or tell her to do it. Instead she sighed and said, "I'll do it."

"Thanks, Em." Grace flashed her sister a relieved smile. "I don't like making salads, and besides, I'm already late because Natalie made me redo all my work this morning. I'm glad it's summer so she isn't telling me to do my homework too."

"Did you do your job right the first time?" Emily gave Grace a knowing look.

"It was good enough," Grace said defensively. "Natalie just likes bossing people."

Emily shifted the heavy bag of feed to her other shoulder. "That isn't fair, Grace, and you know it. Mom put her in charge of the horses, so she needs to make sure everything's done right. She never bosses me."

"That's because you do all your chores and homework without being told. For me, it's always 'Grace, it's time for homework now.' 'Grace, it was your turn to muck those stalls.' All. The. Time."

"That doesn't sound very bossy to me," Emily said, exasperated. "She's just reminding you about things you're supposed to be doing."

Grace stamped her foot. "Em, do you always have to be so logical? Can't you just say, 'You're right, Grace. Natalie *is* bossy,' for once?"

Emily shook her head. "I can't say that because it isn't true."

Grace huffed. "Even if it isn't true, you could at least say it to make me feel better."

Emily nibbled on her lower lip. "I'm sorry, Grace. I *was* trying to make you feel better."

Well, it isn't working, Grace wanted to say, but Emily's eyes reflected her hurt. Besides, she wasn't angry at Emily.

"I know you were only trying to help," Grace offered. "I'm not mad at you. I'm upset because I'm going to be late." Grace hurried off, grumbling under her breath.

The gray storm cloud hanging over her lifted as soon as she unlatched Miz Ida's gate. As usual, the soothing scent of roses erased the gloom. But something was different. The garden was empty. Grace stopped in surprise. Miz Ida always worked in her garden this time of morning. She hoped nothing was wrong.

She climbed the back steps to the stoop and knocked on the kitchen door. Miz Ida opened it. "Hi,

Grace. Come in, come in." She waved to Grace to enter.

Grace stepped in and shut the door behind her.

"I'm in a tizzy. Roger called a few minutes ago." Miz Ida wrung her hands. "The taxi will be coming at eight tomorrow morning, and there's so much to do."

"I can help. Are you all packed?" Grace asked.

Miz Ida looked close to tears. "No, I've been so busy with other things. And I don't know what to take."

Grace had no idea what Miz Ida should pack. "Do you have Roger's phone number?" After Miz Ida gestured toward the list beside her old-fashioned wall phone, Grace said, "Why don't you go in the bedroom and get out your suitcase? I'll ask Roger what to bring."

"What a good idea." Miz Ida sounded genuinely relieved to hear Grace say as much.

Miz Ida shuffled off, and Grace called Roger.

"Is she all right?" Roger asked.

"She's kind of . . ." Grace stopped herself before she said *a mess* and tried to think of a polite way to say it. Maybe she was learning to think before she spoke, but it was hard. She continued, "I think she's going to be okay. But she's worried about getting everything done."

After Grace hung up the phone, she went to find Miz Ida in the bedroom. Miz Ida was sitting on a chair beside her nightstand, and a suitcase lay open on the bed with Chances curled up inside.

"I have a list from Roger," Grace said.

"Thank you, dear." Miz Ida slowly rose from her chair. "Getting this packing done will be one thing off my mind." She squared her shoulders as if she meant business.

"First you need, um . . ." Roger hadn't mentioned this, but it was the first thing Mrs. Ramirez insisted they pack when they went anywhere. Grace couldn't look at Miz Ida, so she kept her head down and mumbled, "Underwear."

"What's that, dear?" Miz Ida looked confused. "Speak up. I can't hear you."

Her face blazing hotter than the afternoon sun, Grace repeated the word. This time it came out so loud, it echoed around the room.

"No need to shout," Miz Ida said. She reached into a dresser drawer and pulled out a quilted pink bag. "I keep a lingerie bag for travel in the back of this drawer."

Grace turned her back while Miz Ida filled the pockets. The *zzzst* of the zipper closing let Grace know when it was safe to turn around. Miz Ida handed her the silk pouch, and Grace shooed Chances out of the suitcase. The cat stalked off with a loud *mrrowww*.

Helping Miz Ida took a lot of patience. Grace chewed at the inside of her lip as Miz Ida spread each piece of clothing on the bed and folded it with precise motions, smoothing it with swollen and shaky fingers after each fold. If it didn't turn out precisely right, she shook it out and started again. Grace was tempted to demonstrate her own *toss-it-in-as-fast-as-you-can* technique, but she suspected Miz Ida might not appreciate arriving at Roger's with wrinkled clothes.

Once the packing was done, Grace put Miz Ida's medications for that evening and tomorrow into small pill cups and tucked the rest into the zippered suitcase pocket. Then she helped Miz Ida put toiletries into a clear plastic bag for her carry-on. When they were done and Grace had placed both bags by the front door for the next day, Miz Ida sank into her usual chair in the living room.

Grace offered to get her a drink, and Miz Ida accepted with a look of relief. When Grace returned with the drinks, Miz Ida sipped hers and appeared a little less shaky, prompting Grace to ask her if she'd eaten anything.

Miz Ida stared up at the ceiling. "You know, I've been so busy, I forgot to eat breakfast."

"Maybe that's why you're worried," Grace said. "Mom always says you can't think clearly if you don't have a good breakfast." Grace stood and headed for the kitchen. "I'll make you a sandwich." Grace was hungry, too, so she made two sandwiches and carried the plates to the living room.

After she'd eaten, Miz Ida seemed a bit more alert, so Grace finally brought up the reason why she'd come over.

"You were going to show me the jobs I need to do while you're away," Grace told her, pulling the crumpled list from her pocket and handing it to her.

"Of course." Miz Ida smoothed out the list. She handed Grace the pen and tablet from the end table beside her and went over each item while Grace took notes. The more she talked, the firmer her voice grew, and soon she seemed almost back to her usual self.

"Chances is the most important thing to remember." Miz Ida pushed on the chair arms to lift herself to her feet. "Let's go into Chances's room now so I can show you some things."

Miz Ida had devoted the back bedroom entirely to Chances. The walls were covered in ribbons and shelves holding trophies, proof that Miz Ida wasn't bragging when she claimed that Chances was a grand champion. Grace always loved coming into the room to stare at the shiny silver, gold, and crystal cups and trophies. Scattered between them were engraved trays and acrylic plaques and lots of ribbons. For the center of the wall, Miz Ida had an artist design a fancy pedigree chart decorated with filigree and paw prints.

"I usually dust these every three days or so," Miz Ida said, "but it can wait until I get back."

Grace blew out a breath. She hadn't looked forward to that job. What if she knocked one over and dented or broke it?

She helped Miz Ida clean the litter box, although she did that plenty of times at home for the rescue cats. She already knew where Chances's toys and grooming tools were stored. She smiled at Chances, who had followed them into the room and curled into her favorite spot—a scratching post with platforms, made from a real tree trunk. It would be fun having the cat all to herself for two weeks.

Miz Ida moved through the rest of the list rapidly, showing Grace where the cat food was stored in the pantry, where she kept the gardening tools and soapy spray for the rosebushes, and where she stored the plant food and fertilizer.

"I think that's everything," Miz Ida said after she explained about watering the herbs and turning the compost. "I did forget to mention one thing. Barbara will only be coming on Thursdays the next two weeks, but she has a key to let herself in."

Grace nodded. Barbara was Miz Ida's cleaning lady. Glancing at the pages of notes in her hands overwhelmed Grace. What if she forgot something? Made a mistake? Ruined something? Maybe she shouldn't have agreed to do this job.

"You look worried," Miz Ida said.

"I am," Grace admitted as she gathered her notes together. "So many things could go wrong."

Miz Ida walked her to the door. "Mistakes can be fixed."

Grace wished that were true, but it seemed she often made ones that were almost impossible to fix.

Chapter Seven

Natalie and Emily were still on the trail ride when Grace got home, and Abby had gone to her friend Miriam's house for the afternoon. Mr. Ramirez was on the phone and signaled for her to keep quiet. The house seemed so lonely without people to talk to. Grace wandered from room to room, stopping to give Amigo, Abby's retired service dog, a pat on the head. She debated about going back to Miz Ida's to pick the vegetables, but instead she grabbed her soccer ball.

While she was practicing dribbling and shooting, a silver convertible zipped into the driveway. A tall man wearing a baseball cap with a bull embroidered on it slid out of the car as she finished driving toward the net. He stood and watched as she drilled a shot into the top left corner of the net.

He applauded. "Terrific shot."

Grace grinned. "Thanks. Can I help you?" she asked, searching for her father in the window. Mr. Ramirez waved to her, giving her the okay to go on without him.

The man nodded. "I heard you have an emu here. I'd be happy to take it off your hands."

"Wow, that would be awesome. My dad's on the

phone right now, but I can take your name and number so he can give you a call."

"Tell you what—why don't I just stop by later and pick it up?" He gestured toward his shiny silver sports car. "Can't picture it sitting there." He threw back his head and chortled.

Grace laughed politely. "That should be fine."

"So we have a deal?" He stuck out a hand, and Grace, not sure what else to do, shook it.

"Sure," she agreed. Emily might be sad to lose the emu, which she'd named Chandler, but Grace would be happy to get rid of that scary bird.

"I'll stop by a little later with my horse trailer. That be all right?" When Grace nodded, he got back in the car. "Emu oil, here we come," he said to himself.

"Emus make oil?" Grace asked.

"Of course," the man said, revving his engine. "Great for cosmetics and stuff. See you later!" He waved and zoomed out of the driveway.

Grace turned when she heard Natalie's voice in the distance.

"Who was that, Grace?" Natalie called.

Grace ran to meet her sisters, back from their trail ride. "He's going to take the emu," she said to them, excitedly.

Emily's face fell. "I know it's too expensive to feed," she said, "but I wish we could keep it."

Natalie's broad smile revealed how overjoyed she was. "I'm glad my ad worked," she said as she dismounted. "Did he suggest a price? I didn't have time to research what emus usually cost."

Grace's family sometimes gave animals away to good homes, but that man looked like he could afford to pay. "No, but I'm sure he'll pay. He wants it for the oil."

"Oil?" Natalie and Emily shrieked in unison.

Emily put one hand on her hip. "Grace, you are not selling the emu to him, no matter what he pays!"

Grace tried to explain herself. "I already shook on the deal, and—"

Emily interrupted her and snapped, "Did you read any of that information Abby collected?"

Grace had started it, but after the first few paragraphs, her eyes glazed over. "Not yet," she admitted.

"Maybe you should." Emily led her pony into the barn to give it a rubdown. "How do you think they make emu oil?"

Grace followed her. "I was going to ask you about that. I bet Mom would like some."

Emily whirled around. "They get the oil from emu fat." Her voice rose in a screech as she continued, "which means they have to *kill* it!"

Grace had shaken hands on a deal to kill Emily's emu?

Emily and Natalie did not speak to her as they untacked and groomed their horses. It was almost as if they went out of their way to avoid her. Emily was concentrating so hard on currycombing Bluebonnet that she didn't look up or smile when Grace passed. Grace almost skipped feeding the horses so Natalie would call her back to take care of it, but she wasn't sure if getting Natalie to talk to her was worth a scolding. Instead, she did her best at all the jobs.

By the time she finished, Natalie had gone into the house to help Mr. Ramirez start dinner. Grace and Emily were the only ones in the barn when the emu man backed his horse trailer down the driveway.

Grace considered her options. She could hide in here, and maybe if he didn't see anyone, he'd go away. Or she could go out and tell him she was breaking her promise. Or . . .

Before she could think of a third option, Emily, her legs trembling, marched out to meet the man. In a quavering voice, she told him, "There's been a mistake. Our emu is not for sale."

The man's eyebrows rose. "You told me earlier I could have him. We even shook on the deal."

"No, we didn't," Emily said, crossing her arms.

The man tilted back his baseball cap and scratched his head. "Could have sworn we did." Then he caught sight of Grace peeking out from the barn, and he rubbed his eyes. "Am I seeing double?"

Grace wanted to hide and let Emily deal with it, but she'd come up with her third option—admit she made a mistake and try to fix it.

"I'm the one who shook your hand," she said as she approached, "but I shouldn't have. Actually, only my parents are supposed to make the agreements. But as my dad says, 'A deal's a deal,' and we shook hands, so I have to keep my promise."

Beside her, Emily gasped. "No, Grace." She grabbed Grace's arm. "I won't ever, ever ask you to break a promise again, but please don't do this." Emily burst into tears.

Grace held up a finger. "Just a minute, Em." Turning back to the man, she said, "I'll stick to my bargain, but we didn't agree on a price."

"That's true." The man stroked his chin. "Something tells me I'm not going to like this."

"Considering how much my sister loves the emu, I think $50,000 is a fair price."

"What?" The man shook his head. "I might give you a few hundred."

"Our emu is worth more than that," Grace said. "I'm sorry, but that price is firm."

The man shook his head. "That's out of my price range."

As he started toward his horse trailer, Emily called after him, "Please don't buy any more emus." Her voice shook, and tears rolled down her cheeks. "Not for oil."

"Well, now," said the man, turning to face her. "Don't cry. Tell you what. I'll make you a deal. No more emus for me if your dad will agree to a low price on his hay."

This time Grace stood her ground. "I can't speak for my dad, but I'll do my best to get you a good deal."

The man laughed. "You'll be a good negotiator someday." Then he looked at Emily. "Just between us, I've never purchased an emu before. I only heard they bring a good price for meat and oil." He rubbed the back of his neck. "But I found out they can be mean old birds. Friend of mine says they have the kick of a horse and the claws of a wolf, so you be careful."

"You don't have to worry about my sister," Grace informed him. "She has a magic touch with animals. They all love her."

"I'm not surprised. She seems to care deeply about them. But as for you . . ." He studied Grace.

Grace wanted to cover her ears. *Even a stranger can tell I don't measure up to Emily,* she thought. *Being a good negotiator is not the same as loving animals.*

The man continued, "You're not only a good soccer player and great negotiator, I can tell you're good with people."

"Yes, she is," Emily agreed. "She's always helping our neighbor, and she's not afraid to talk to people."

Grace hadn't felt fearless when she'd been cowering in the barn, letting Emily do the talking, but she appreciated her sister's support.

"Being brave is important," the man said. "Now I hope you'll put your negotiating skills to good use with your dad." He winked and then waved as he headed toward his truck.

As he pulled his horse trailer out of the drive-way, Emily threw her arms around Grace's neck and hugged her.

"Thank you, thank you!" Emily squealed. "You saved Chandler."

Grace hugged her back, relieved that horse trailer wasn't pulling out with Chandler inside. If that man had taken Chandler, that would have been one mistake she'd never be able to fix. She'd been lucky this time. But from now on, she needed to stop and think before she rushed into things.

That is, if she could remember . . .

Chapter Eight

Grace hadn't realized how much work taking care of Miz Ida's house and garden would be. Miz Ida had been gone almost a week, and the soaring temperatures were threatening to kill the plants. She had to water them early in the morning and then again later in the day.

Miz Ida always sprayed a small test spray on her hand before turning the hose on the plants, but Grace was in a hurry to get all the chores done. She directed the nozzle at the first row and squeezed the trigger. A powerful jet of water flattened a whole row of plants. *Oh, no.* She must have accidentally twisted the pressure ring. She knelt and tried to fix them, but they lay broken and battered.

Then she walked through the kitchen to feed Chances and noticed the herbs on the windowsill were brown and drooping. She'd forgotten all about them. While Chances wove around her ankles yowling for her breakfast, Grace watered each pot, but she was worried it might be too late.

The next morning when Grace entered Miz Ida's gate, a smell of rotten eggs wafted from the garden. *The compost pile!* She hadn't been turning it. She hurried over, lifted the lid of the bin, and gagged. Everything was wet and super slimy.

Grace wanted to cry. Weeds were overtaking the garden. She'd ruined the compost pile, killed the herbs on the kitchen windowsill, and squished a row of plants. What would Miz Ida think when she returned?

That night, after a long, hot day in the sun, she fell into bed exhausted. She slept fitfully, worried about Miz Ida's disappointment.

Aarrooo.

Grace jolted awake. She was breathing fast. It was a coyote. Grace had lived in the city until she was six, so she still sometimes found the strange sounds out here on the ranch unnerving. In addition to the noises from their own rescue animals, neighboring ranches contributed braying and bleating and lowing to the cacophony. Worst of all, wild animals like frogs and owls added their own *wop-wop*s, *whirr*s, ghostly *ooohh*s, rustling, trilling, squeaking, screeching, and growling. Eeriest of all was that coyote's howl, which sent chills down her back. Grace pulled the sheet up to her chin as if it could protect her.

Most of the nature sounds in the Texas country-side were more soothing than the constant roar of

traffic, honking cars, and screaming sirens of her city home, but Grace missed the hustle and bustle of city streets, being surrounded by crowds of people, and constant action. And most of all, she missed her first mom. Her birth mom.

Moving here had been hard, and Grace used to wake at night disoriented after dreaming she was back in their tiny Dallas apartment. Back when it was just her and Emily and their mother. By now she had learned to call her mother's college friend, Teresa Ramirez, "Mom," but there was still a part of Grace's heart that belonged to her birth mother, and there always would be. Her mom had raised her and Emily alone after their dad died in a car accident when they were babies. Teresa had come to help when their mother went into hospice, and she'd taken Grace and Emily back to the ranch after the funeral. Teresa had been their godmother, and their mother's will had made Teresa their guardian. The Ramirez family adopted them soon after they moved from Dallas to Sugarberry.

Grace wished Emily were awake so she would have someone to talk to, someone who remembered their birth mother, someone to ease the loneliness. When they were little, she and Emily shared a bed in their tiny apartment, and their mother slept on the sofa. If only she were still young enough to have someone close for comfort.

She slipped out of bed and stood over Emily, wishing her sister would open her eyes. Maybe they could sneak down to the kitchen and share a cup of hot chocolate. Emily's chest rose and fell with such slow, even breaths, Grace hesitated to wake her. She trudged down to the kitchen alone.

After she'd poured milk in a mug and heated it in the microwave, Grace couldn't find any packets of hot chocolate. She'd have to drink warm milk instead.

As she passed through the living room, carrying her mug of milk, a light flickered outside the window, and she stopped short. It had been a small flare, not like car headlights that shone bright, steady, and low to the ground. She gulped a mouthful of milk while she waited for another flash. There it came again. Only this time the pinpoint of light reappeared and moved steadily behind a window.

Miz Ida's window! Someone was inside her house.

Slamming her mug down on the coffee table, Grace raced to the front door. She was responsible for Miz Ida's house. She had to get over there. One hand on the doorknob, she recalled her disasters with bareback riding and almost selling the emu. She'd made a decision to think ahead. Although she was only going across the street, she'd better tell Emily. If Emily woke and saw Grace's bed empty, she'd panic.

Irritated about the amount of time she was losing, Grace climbed the stairs two at a time and rushed into the bedroom and to her sister's bed. "Emily, wake up!" she whispered as she shook her sister's shoulder.

Emily batted away Grace's hand, buried her head under the covers, and rolled over. "*Mmmrff.*"

Grace gave the covers a yank, and they sailed onto the floor.

Emily wrapped her arms around herself. "Leave me alone," she whimpered.

"Please, Emily," Grace begged, keeping her voice low so she wouldn't wake her parents or older sisters. "I have to go. I think someone is robbing Miz Ida's."

Her sister shot up in bed, her eyes wide open. "Are you sure?"

Grace nodded. "Someone's inside with a flashlight. I wanted you to know where I'm going."

"No way am I letting you go out there alone." Emily hopped out of bed. "Um, Grace," Emily said as Grace dashed for the door. "Were you planning to go out there in your pajamas?"

Grace didn't want to waste any more time, but Emily was right. Her bright white sleep shirt and shorts weren't the best for spying. Besides being embarrassed if any of the neighbors saw her, she'd be spotted by whoever was sneaking around in Miz Ida's house.

"But the burglar may get away if we wait," Grace said.

Emily ignored her and pulled out a navy blue hoodie and dark leggings. Yanking open her bottom dresser drawer, Grace rifled through her clothes, tossing unneeded ones into heaps on the floor. While Grace was digging, Emily pocketed her cell phone and a flashlight. Emily never went anywhere without her cell phone because she was always snapping pictures. Finally, Grace unearthed a black hoodie to cover her blond hair and wiggled into a pair of jeans. She pocketed Miz Ida's key.

As Grace galloped down the stairs, Emily whispered, "We should tell Mom and Dad."

"No way," Grace said, shaking her head vehemently. "They'd never let us go, but I promised Miz Ida I'd keep an eye on her house."

Emily's heavy sigh sounded disapproving, but she trailed Grace out the door and did her best to keep up. By the time Grace raced across their front yard and reached the road, Emily was huffing behind her. No cars would be out this late at night, but Grace stopped for a second to glance both ways before sprinting across the road and up Miz Ida's long driveway. She reached the bushes beside Miz Ida's house long before Emily.

By the time Emily arrived, gasping for air, Grace was already on tiptoes, peering in the window.

"This is where I saw the light," Grace whispered to Emily. "No one's in there now."

She shouldn't have waited. If she'd dashed over here right away, she might have caught the intruder. Maybe thinking before acting wasn't always the best idea.

"Which window? Did you look in?" Emily asked, coming up behind her, still out of breath. The driveway up to Miz Ida's house was a long one.

"This one. It's Miz Ida's bedroom," Grace said.

The curtains blocked some of the view, but a flashlight would be visible through them. They'd need to check the other windows.

"We should split up and peek in the other windows." Grace turned to Emily. "Could you breathe quieter?"

"I'll . . . try," Emily said between huffs. "But I think . . . we should . . . stay . . . together."

Grace tried not to let her annoyance show. Emily was such a scaredy-cat sometimes. "Come on, then,"

Grace said and trotted around to the front of the house.

After checking the living room and dining room windows and finding nothing, Grace hurried to the opposite side of the house. The bathroom window had glazed blocks. Grace wasn't sure if light would show through those, but a burglar probably wouldn't be looking in there anyway. The next window down, Miz Ida's guest bedroom, appeared empty, but when they rounded the house to the garden fence, Grace skidded to a stop.

"Look, Em. Someone's definitely here." Grace pointed to an old rusty truck, partially hidden by the trees beside the garden fence. Whoever was in the house must still be there.

Emily nodded and whipped out her cell phone. She snapped a picture of the license plate and one of the truck. It hadn't occurred to Grace to do that. Maybe thinking instead of just acting was a good thing sometimes.

While Emily was taking pictures, Grace put her hand on the latch to open the garden gate, but the gate was already slightly ajar. This must be the way the burglar had come in. She motioned for her sister to follow her.

They tiptoed toward the closest back window, Chances's trophy room. A light flashed in an odd circular motion. They'd found the burglar. Grace started toward the window, but Emily grabbed her arm and held on so tightly her fingernails dug into Grace's skin.

Grace tried to shake her off. "Let go, Em," she snapped in a low voice. "I have to see what's happening."

Trembling from head to toe, Emily refused to let go. "What if the burglar sees you? He could be dangerous. And look, the back door's partway open. He could come out any minute." Although she was quiet, Emily was firm. "Now that we know someone's in there, we should call 911."

As usual, Emily was right, but Grace wanted to catch the burglar red-handed. Her sister pulled out her cell, but Grace swatted at her hand before she could hit any buttons. "The burglar might see the light," she hissed and pointed to the gate.

Emily nodded and slipped outside the gate. As soon as her sister had gone, Grace stood on tiptoe and peeked in the window. A man dressed all in black stood with his back to her, his flashlight circling around the wall of trophies and ribbons. He snatched a few and then took down Chances's framed pedigree chart and shoved them into a lumpy cloth bag on the floor beside him.

Grace's fists knotted. He had no right to steal Chances's awards. She pinched her lips shut to keep from shouting at him. She couldn't let him know she was there, but she had to find a way to stop him.

Chapter Nine

As the man moved, his flashlight bobbed up and down. The beam of light shone briefly on Chances curled up in her cat bed. Grace breathed a sigh of relief. At least Chances was safe.

The man grabbed a few more trophies and stuffed them in his bag. While he was bent over, Chances stretched, padded over, and climbed her scratching-post tree. Then she leapt. Right on his back. With a yowl, she kneaded her claws into his shirt.

The man tumbled to the floor, batting at her with one arm and trying to push himself to his feet with the other. Chances reached out a paw and swiped at the back of his neck. Those claws had raked Grace's ankles before, so Grace knew it must have hurt.

Shouting and swearing loudly enough to be heard through the glass, the burglar grabbed for the back of his neck. He stumbled to his feet and jerked back and forth, trying to shake Chances off, but the cat clung on with three paws while swiping at him with her right front paw.

Go, Chances! Grace thought.

The man twisted and turned, but Chances scratched his hands each time he reached back to grab her. He danced around, shaking his hand in the

air, and Grace couldn't help giggling. She pressed a hand over her mouth to muffle the sound.

She stopped snickering when the man picked up the bag and knocked Chances off his back. Grace clenched her teeth to keep from screaming. At least Chances landed on her feet. She yowled and then retreated into the corner to lick her paws.

The man grabbed the cat carrier, opened the door, and slid it toward Chances. With one quick shove, the man pushed her inside and latched it. Chances yowled and banged at the locked door.

Grace's rage boiled over. She wanted to pound on the window and yell. Rush in and tackle the catnapper. Grab the cat carrier with Chances in it. Without thinking, she started toward the back door. She had to get Chances away from him somehow.

Someone grabbed Grace's arm from behind and she swallowed her yelp, turning it into a strangled gurgle.

"Emily, you scared me to death," Grace choked out. "I thought you were another burglar."

Emily got close enough to whisper in Grace's ear in a shaky voice, "At first 911 thought it was a prank call, but I convinced them we really did see a burglar. They're sending some officers to check it out. They said we need to get out of here right away. The police will take care of it." She grabbed Grace's arm to drag her away.

"He already has Chances in a carrier. They might not get here in time to catch him," Grace whispered back. "I have an idea on how to slow him down."

The kitchen door was slightly ajar, so he'd be coming out that way. No way would Grace let the burglar escape.

Emily was practically crying. "Don't do anything foolish," she begged.

Grace broke free of her sister's grasp and sprinted to the back steps, snatched the empty plastic bucket, and dashed back to the garden plot. No matter what happened to her, she had to save Chances. Grace dipped the bucket in the slimy compost, ran over to the concrete steps, dumped the contents all over the stoop, and dribbled the rest down the steps.

When she raced back toward the garden again, Emily caught up with her. This time tears were running down her face. "Don't, Grace! It's too dangerous!"

Emily tried to drag Grace toward the open gate, but Grace resisted. Grace wriggled free and flew toward the garden. "Go stand out front and watch for the police. Direct them back here."

"Come with me," Emily pleaded.

Grace shook her head, grabbed another bucketful of compost, and sloshed it over the walkway at the bottom of the steps.

"If you want to help me, flag down the police." Grace ducked into the bushes closest to the back door.

The branches pricked and poked her, but she wiggled in as deep as she could so she was hidden from view. She'd get a description of the man for the police. Her arms were scratched and bleeding by the time she'd found a place where she could see without being seen. If the catnapper heard rustling in the bushes, she hoped he'd assume it was an animal. Sirens sounded in the distance, and Grace hoped they'd turn them off so they wouldn't alert the catnapper.

The door squeaked open. The catnapper peeked out to the left and then to the right before stepping onto the porch. His shoes hit the slippery muck, and with a loud scream, he slid across the porch. Desperate to keep his balance, he windmilled his arms but kept skidding right over the edge of the stoop and bumped down the steps. The cat carrier shot out of his hands, and Grace's heart stutter-stopped as it somersaulted through the air.

Chances!

Higher and higher it went, tumbling over, then plunging down. Inside, Chances's yowls turned to high-pitched screeches.

If Grace's plan hurt or killed Chances, she'd never forgive herself.

Chapter Ten

Clunk! **The cat carrier** landed above Grace's head, crushing the bushes. Twigs ripped and tore at Grace's arms and legs as she tumbled backward.

"Grace!" Emily screamed behind her.

"Don't move!" a deep voice commanded. "Hands in the air!"

Grace got to her feet and automatically raised her hands. Then she realized the police were talking to the catnapper. Sheepishly, she lowered her hands, hoping no one had seen her.

Two officers rushed toward the man, and one handcuffed him. Lights from the police car flashed, lighting up the night.

As they led him away, Grace gently lifted the cat carrier and set it on the ground. Chances had been silent ever since the carrier landed in the bushes. Fearing the worst, Grace lay on her stomach and opened the door, not caring that she was getting wet and slimy. She reached a hand inside, and a hissing, spitting, scratching, soaking-wet bundle of fur came streaking out. As Chances escaped, her claws raked across Grace's hand, drawing more blood, but Grace didn't care. The cat was alive.

Emily came up behind Grace. "Is Chances all right?" she asked, her voice trembling.

The officers had left the garden gate open. Grace hightailed it over there and slammed it right before Chances reached it.

"I beat you by a whisker," Grace wheezed. "Now you can either let me hold you, or you can go back in that cat carrier. Which is it going to be?" She approached Chances with her hands out.

With a yowl, Chances took off. Grace waited until the Persian calmed, then scooped her up. She stroked her wet fur. "It's all right," Grace whispered to Chances over and over. "I'm taking you home with me tonight," she said to the cat, now calmed. She'd just reached the gate again when it opened, and an officer strode through.

"Come with me," the officer said, putting one heavy hand on Grace's shoulder and another on Emily's. Photographers snapped pictures of the cat-napper as the police officer marched the girls past the patrol car. "Now, where do you two live?"

Emily was still very shaken, so Grace shifted Chances to point out their ranch.

"I'll see that you get there. Once you're home, I want you to remain inside for the rest of the night." She looked at each girl in turn. "Do you understand?"

The officer walked the girls across the road and knocked on their door. After a brief wait, Mrs.

Ramirez opened it wearing a sweatshirt over her pajamas, her hair in disarray.

"Grace? Emily?" She stared at the officer, confused.

"Ma'am, we found these two across the street," the police officer said. "They indicated that they live here."

"Yes, yes, they do. They're my daughters." Mrs. Ramirez kept her gaze steady while the officer appraised her and then the two girls.

The officer glanced away first. "There's been a burglary at that residence," she said, waving toward Miz Ida's house, "so I'd appreciate it if you'd keep a close eye on them. We don't want them anywhere near the crime scene."

"Crime scene?" Mrs. Ramirez shrieked. She looked as if she were about to faint.

"Yes, one of our officers will be by tomorrow to take their statements."

"Statements?" Mrs. Ramirez shook her head, then turned to face Grace.

Why did their mom look at Grace first? She didn't even seem to consider that Emily had done anything wrong—only Grace. Of course, she was right.

"Do you know how we can reach the homeowner?" the officer asked.

"Miz Ida has a list by the kitchen phone," Grace answered, still stroking Chances's head. "She's staying with her son, Roger. His number's at the top."

"I understand you have a key, so we can lock up when we're done." The officer held out a hand.

Grace reached into the pocket of her hoodie. It was empty. "The key must have fallen out when I fell. I have to go get it."

"You'll do no such thing," Mrs. Ramirez barked. "Not tonight you aren't."

"No worries, ma'am. I know where she fell. We'll look for the key and return it tomorrow." The officer pinned Grace with a warning look as the girls and Chances filed into the house.

Mrs. Ramirez closed the door behind the officer, then turned to face Grace and Emily. "What in the world is going on?" She held up a hand. "Wait, maybe Dad should hear this too."

A banging on the door made Mrs. Ramirez jump. She turned and opened the door.

"*Sugarberry News*, ma'am." The man held out his ID. "I'd like to talk to the little girl who helped catch the burglar."

"Not tonight." Mrs. Ramirez closed the door while the man continued shouting questions at Grace.

Mr. Ramirez came into the room, rubbing his eyes. "What's all this noise?" he asked.

"It seems our daughters were somehow involved with a burglary," Mrs. Ramirez replied.

"What?" Mr. Ramirez staggered over to a chair and sank into it. "Okay, someone tell me what's going on." He, too, looked straight at Grace rather than Emily. "Have a seat."

The girls sat on the couch. Grace launched into the story while continuing to smooth Chances's matted fur. Emily added bits here and there.

When they were done, Mr. Ramirez said, "I'm proud of your bravery, Grace, but—"

"Hector, don't encourage her," Mrs. Ramirez interrupted, pressing two fists against her chest and turning a searching look on Grace. "Are you trying to give us heart attacks?"

Mr. Ramirez shook his head. "Teresa, she's only nine."

"Nine is old enough to think of the consequences," Mrs. Ramirez snapped.

Grace hung her head. "I'm sorry. I've been trying hard to think before I act, but sometimes my ideas run away with me."

Chances jumped from Grace's lap to chase a moth, and Mrs. Ramirez glanced at Grace's hands. "Is that blood?" Mrs. Ramirez asked, concerned. She stood and pointed down the hall. "Into the bathroom right now."

The bright light in the bathroom revealed Grace's hands and arms were crisscrossed with cuts and scratches, some superficial, some deep and bleeding. Mrs. Ramirez rinsed Grace's arms thoroughly with antiseptic wash and patted them dry. Then she slathered them with ointment. "I know it's warm, but put on a long-sleeved cotton top to protect your arms tonight," Mrs. Ramirez told her daughter.

"Can you also check Chances to be sure she's okay?" Grace asked.

Mrs. Ramirez did a thorough examination and pronounced Chances perfectly fine. "Cats usually do land on their feet. She's lucky nothing happened to her."

And even luckier that the carrier had landed in the bushes. If that hadn't cushioned her fall, who knows what might have happened. Grace never wanted to go through something like that again. An image of Chances's cage catapulting through the air should be enough of a reminder to think things through.

A few reporters began knocking on the door early the next morning, begging to interview Grace. Mrs. Ramirez sent them all away and brought in a copy of the *Sugarberry News* with the headline, "Nine-Year-Old Foils Cat Burglar." The story made Grace sound like a hero. Natalie and Abby read the newspaper but still wanted to hear the whole story from Grace.

After she finished, Natalie said, "Wow, Grace, I don't think I'd ever be that brave. I would have run the other way."

"Me too," Abby said.

"You would have?" Grace asked. Had she really been that brave?

"Are Miz Ida's steps still slimed?" Natalie asked.

Grace nodded. "Mom won't let me go over there alone, so I can't clean it up, and I messed up on a lot of the jobs Miz Ida wanted me to do. She's not going to be very happy when she gets home." Grace had no idea how she'd explain all of this to Miz Ida. Almost-dead herbs, empty compost bin, unweeded garden, slimed-up steps, and a burglary—all in under a week.

"Let's all go over when we're finished with our chores," Natalie suggested. "It won't take long if all four of us help."

"Are you sure?" Grace couldn't believe Natalie was offering to help at Miz Ida's.

"Of course," Natalie said. "We're a family, right?" Emily and Abby nodded in agreement. The girls finished their breakfast and hurried out to care for the animals.

When all four sisters had finished, the girls and Chances went to Miz Ida's.

"What do we need to do, Grace?" Natalie asked.

Hmmm. Maybe Emily was right. Perhaps Natalie wasn't as bossy as Grace thought. She was letting Grace be the boss here. Grace assigned everyone jobs, and she did what Natalie always did when she gave out chores—saved the hardest one for herself. Soon

Natalie and Emily were weeding, Abby was caring for Chances and tending the herbs on the windowsill, and Grace was scrubbing and hosing down the stinky slime on the steps and walkway.

"Hey, Grace," Abby came to the doorway. "I found this on the floor of Chances's room." She held up the pedigree painting.

It must have fallen out of the bag when the burglar was trying to get Chances off his back. Grace cleaned off her shoes and went inside to hang the painting. Then she rearranged the wall display so the missing items didn't appear as noticeable.

By the time Miz Ida arrived by taxi, everything had been restored to order. Grace was surprised to see her home early, but Miz Ida had taken the first flight home once she had heard the news. Grace repeated the whole story again, and Miz Ida sat shaking her head.

"I'm not sure whether to lecture you or praise you," Miz Ida said. "I'm sure you know how dangerous that was. But thank you for caring for Chances." She reached into her purse. "Here's the money I owe you."

Grace shook her head. "I don't deserve it. I messed up the garden and the herbs and . . ." Grace trailed off and bit her lip.

Miz Ida closed Grace's fingers around the money. "You may have done something foolhardy, but your heart was in the right place. Consider it reward money for catching the catnapper." She winked, then let out a long breath. "Traveling makes me sleepy, so I'm going to take a nap. Come by tomorrow, Grace dear. I have some news."

The way Miz Ida's lips pinched together, it didn't look like it would be good news.

At home, Grace divided the money into four equal parts and handed one to each of her sisters, but they all refused to take it.

"We only helped one day," Natalie said. "You did the rest. Keep the money."

If her sisters wouldn't take the money, Grace had another idea. She asked Mr. Ramirez to bring her into town, and he promised to take her that afternoon. Grace grew antsy waiting for him to finish all the small jobs around the ranch, but she reminded herself it was a chance to practice patience.

When they finally reached town, Mr. Ramirez warned, "Don't spend all that money in one place. Might be good to save some."

Grace didn't plan to spend all of it. When she got home, she set a gift by each person's place at the table—a dog encyclopedia for Abby, an art set for Emily, a set of breakdown barrels for Natalie, and a gift certificate for a massage for Mrs. Ramirez. She had a hard time finding something for Mr. Ramirez though. In the end she chose a tool set and a mug that said "World's Greatest Dad." She also handed him the rest of the money to put in her savings account.

Grace enjoyed everyone's pleased reactions to her thank-you gifts when they gathered at the dinner table that night, but her mind kept returning to Miz Ida. What news had made her look so sad?

Chapter Eleven

Grace sat stunned after hearing Miz Ida's news. "You're going away for good?"

She tried to picture the house without Miz Ida in it. Other than the trip to her son's house, Miz Ida had always been there for her. From the time Grace and Emily arrived on the ranch, Miz Ida had been Grace's listening ear, her best friend after her twin sister. Miz Ida had held Grace when she'd cried over her mother's death, understood her loneliness, and soothed her hurt feelings. She'd cared about Grace's problems and taught her to garden. They'd shared lemonade and secrets.

And now she'd be moving? Going away forever?

Grace struggled to wrap her mind around it. "I don't want you to go. I'll miss you." She got up from the chair and flung her arms around Miz Ida.

Miz Ida laughed, then wheezed out, "Don't squeeze the breath out of me, child." Her words sounded like scolding, but she had tears in her eyes. "I'll miss you, too, Grace. You've been a wonderful friend."

"You always say to think ahead," Grace said.

"Yes, indeedy, I do," Miz Ida agreed. "And I *have* been considering my options. That's why I went to my son's. I love being here with you, and I'm happy in

my own house and garden, but caring for everything
is getting too much for me."

"If you stay, I could help," Grace said. "I could do
all the gardening for you and keep an eye on you and
help you. That's an option."

"Oh, Grace, that's so sweet of you, and I'd love
to take you up on that. But the house needs a lot of
work, and I miss being near my son and my grand-
children. Traveling's hard on these old bones." Miz
Ida patted her leg.

Grace could hardly push the words past the lump in her throat. "So you really are moving to Arizona?"

"Yes, dear. I'll be putting the house up for sale this week." Miz Ida said.

"So . . . so I won't be able to garden with you anymore," Grace said.

Miz Ida handed her a tall, cool glass of lemonade. "Maybe the new owners will need help with the garden, but I'll tell you what—why don't I give you some cuttings so you can start your own garden?" With a sly smile, Miz Ida added, "I'd offer you some compost, but I'm afraid I don't have much left."

Grace giggled. "I'm sorry about that."

"I'm not," Miz Ida said. "It helped save Chances." She sipped her sweet tea, then said, "Speaking of Chances, I have a problem. My son's allergic to cats, so I have to sell her."

Grace almost blurted out that she'd buy the cat, but she was trying hard to think before she acted. "How much will she cost?"

When Miz Ida told her the price, Grace's eyes popped open. She had no idea cats cost that much. They got all their cats on the ranch for free when their owners couldn't care for them properly. She was glad she hadn't offered to buy Chances. Where would she get that much money?

Setting her lemonade on a coaster, Miz Ida picked up a pen and tablet from the end table. "That's a bargain price for a championship cat people can breed. And she's been in a few commercials, so she'll make good money for her owners."

Grace sat there, stunned. She loved Chances, and she hated to think of the cat going to another family. It was hard enough losing Miz Ida, but to lose Chances too? Her whole insides ached at the thought.

"I should write the ad and send it in." Miz Ida tapped the end of the pen against her lip. "What should I say?"

Together Miz Ida and Grace came up with the wording for the ad. Then Grace helped Miz Ida post it online. While Miz Ida paid for the ad, Grace strolled into Chances's award room, her eyes blurred with tears. Would the new owner take all these ribbons and cups?

Chances lay in the sunshine on one of the lower platforms on her scratching-post tree, one of her favorite places to curl up. Grace sank onto the floor beside her and ran a hand through her long, silky fur.

"I'm glad I saved you, Chances," she whispered, "but I didn't know that after this week I'd never see you again."

Miz Ida came to the doorway and looked at the two of them. "It's going to be so hard to part with her. And I'm going to miss you, Grace."

Grace turned her head in Chances's direction so Miz Ida couldn't see the tears in her eyes. "I'll miss both of you too," Grace said, her voice cracking. The ache inside Grace grew so large it pressed against her chest and made her ribs hurt. What would she do without them?

Chapter Twelve

Miz Ida had asked Grace to help her interview possible owners for Chances, so the following day, Grace headed across the road, a notebook tucked under her arm. She remembered to look both ways. She'd been working hard to follow Miz Ida's advice on thinking before acting. She only wished she could get Miz Ida to reconsider her decision. The *For Sale* sign on the front lawn hit Grace like a punch in the gut. Shoulders slumped, she walked to the front door instead of the garden.

Miz Ida smiled at her and opened the door wide. "Come in. You look very businesslike today, Grace."

Grace had watched Abby make lists and match people with Cocoa's puppies. One man had insisted he wanted Clove, but Abby asked questions and studied the man's personality. Then she steered the man to a different puppy that was a better fit. Grace wanted to be like Abby and find the best owner for Chances.

The first lady to arrive held her little daughter's hand. The little girl jumped up and down. "Where's kitty?" she demanded.

Miz Ida invited them in and introduced Grace as "my assistant." Grace sat up straighter and tried to look grown-up and efficient.

"Grace will be helping with the interviews today," Miz Ida said, motioning for the lady to sit on the sofa. "We both want to make sure Chances goes to the very best home, so we've scheduled three interviews today."

"*Hmmph.* I thought we were just coming to pick up a cat. I don't know if I have enough time for an interview. I have a nail appointment at 10, and Madeleine's nanny is meeting me there ten minutes before."

"I'll keep it brief," Grace said. She'd heard

Mr. Ramirez say that to people, and it sounded businesslike.

Miz Ida rewarded her with a wink and a smile.

Before Grace could ask the first question, though, Madeleine squirmed off the couch. "I want kitty now," she demanded. "Where's kitty?"

Chances crawled out from under the couch to bat the lady's ankle. She shrieked and jumped to her feet. "Something bit me."

"It was only Chances batting at your leg," Grace said. "She likes to sneak up on people."

The lady examined her ankle. "That cat left scratch marks. We'll have to have her declawed right away."

Horrified, Grace wrote in her notebook under the lady's name:

Declaw Chances? No way

Spoiled daughter

"How old is your daughter?" Grace asked as Madeleine got down on her stomach and peeked under the couch.

Before Grace could stop her, the little girl grabbed a handful of fur and yanked. Chances swiped a paw at her, and Madeleine yelled, "Bad kitty."

"Don't worry, darling, we'll get a trainer to teach the cat proper manners. No more of this sneaking around stuff." She stood and reached for her daughter's hand. "I need to go, but I want to be sure of three things before I buy: that she's a grand champion, that she has a good pedigree, and that she's pure white. I want her to look good when our home is photographed for *Luxury Homes* magazine."

When Miz Ida confirmed these things, the woman pulled out her checkbook. "I'll give you a deposit and have our chauffeur stop by later this afternoon."

Miz Ida held up a hand. "We have two more interviews before we make our decision."

"Well, I'm certain you'll agree we can provide a lovely home. Do give me a call when you've decided on us." She dropped her checkbook back in her purse and swept out the door, towing a crying Madeleine, who kept repeating, "I want kitty."

When the door closed behind them, Miz Ida raised her eyebrows but didn't say a word.

Grace shook her head. "She didn't even look at the cat." She added more items to her list:

Hire a cat trainer?

Doesn't care about cats—wants photo

Chauffeur will pick up cat

And next to *Spoiled daughter*, Grace added, *will hurt Chances!!!!!*

The next interviewee showed up ten minutes early. She strode into the room and demanded to see Chances's pedigree. Miz Ida led her to the trophy room where Chances lay curled on the scratching-post tree in the sunshine. The woman studied Chances closely, and her brows rose when she saw all the awards. Adjusting her glasses, she stepped closer to the framed pedigree chart.

"I assume you also have official paperwork?" the lady said.

"Of course," Miz Ida said. "I had this designed by the well-known artist—"

The lady cut her off. "I'd prefer to peruse the official information."

Miz Ida tottered to a file drawer and removed a folder from it. She handed the folder to the lady.

The lady spent a lot of time examining papers.

Then she nodded. "She'll do, although I must say I'd prefer a different name for showing her. Maybe something like *Precious . . .*" She trailed off, looking at Chances and tapping a thumb against her lip. "Now about the price. I'm willing to pay half of what you're asking."

"Thank you," Miz Ida said, her voice firm as she ushered the lady to the door. "We have another interview shortly."

"I'd be willing to pay up to three-quarters of what you're asking, but that's my final offer," she said as Miz Ida was shutting the front door.

Miz Ida only nodded. As soon as the lady drove off, Miz Ida sank into her favorite hard-backed chair and watched Grace scribbling in her notebook:

Won't pay full price—Cheapskate!!!
Only cares about pedigree
Didn't try to pet Chances
Hates Chances's name

The third interviewee was a man with a big round belly who shuffled into the house and sank on the sofa. Grace sat poised with her pen, ready to take notes. He smiled at her indulgently and then snapped questions at Miz Ida—what was the cat's pedigree, had she ever been bred, how old was she, how was her physical health, did she have any problems, what awards had she won? He seemed satisfied with the answers.

"Did you want to see the cat?" Miz Ida asked when the man stood.

"Of course." The man followed her into trophy room, where Chances lay curled in her usual spot. His eyes fixed on the trophy wall, the man walked right past the cat. He sucked in a breath and then whistled. "That's one prize-winning cat." His eyes gleamed. "Do these awards come with the cat?"

"Of course," Miz Ida assured him. "They belong to Chances. I hope her new owner will want to display them."

The man's eyes gleamed. "Have no fear. I'm more than happy to put them in a prominent place. Now what do I owe you?"

"The cat is over there." Miz Ida's tone was sharp.

"Oh, right." The man strode over to Chances and looked her over. She opened her eyes and stared back. He stepped back a few steps. "Um, she has two different colored eyes." When Chances swiped out at him with her paw, he retreated further.

"Yes," said Grace. "That was in the ad."

"I remember," he said when he stood a safe distance away. "That intrigued me. I'm always looking for rare cats."

Miz Ida walked him to the door. "We'll let everyone know our decision tomorrow after I have a chance to talk things over with my assistant," Miz Ida told the man. She closed the door and leaned her head against it. "I'm exhausted. This has been very draining. It's hard enough having to sell Chances, but finding someone suitable is going to be difficult."

"I know." Grace had not thought any of the people would make suitable owners for Chances. Her list this time said:

Never called Chances by name—only said "the cat"
Doesn't care about Chances
Only wants to make money with breeding
Cares more about awards than Chances
Collects rare cats

Afraid of cats???

"Grace, if you don't mind, I'm going to lie down for a nap." Miz Ida's face appeared pale, and her wrinkles had deepened. "Why don't you stop by tomorrow, and we'll discuss the interviews? I appreciate you taking notes, and I'd like to hear your opinion on which person should get Chances."

Grace closed her notebook with a snap and stood. "Are you sure you're all right? You don't look too good." Then she clapped a hand to her mouth. "I'm sorry. I didn't mean that you look bad. I meant tired. You look tired."

Miz Ida laughed. "I know exactly what you meant. And don't worry, I'll be right as rain tomorrow."

Grace waved good-bye and wandered home, concerned about Miz Ida's decision the next day. None of the people who came seemed right for Chances. She hated thinking about her favorite cat going to any of those homes.

Chapter Thirteen

At dinner when it was her turn to share about her day, ordinarily Grace would have bragged about Miz Ida introducing her as an assistant, but tonight all her thoughts centered on Chances's future. She recounted the interviews and ended by saying, "I hate the thought of any of them having her. All I want to do is snatch up Chances and run far, far away so none of them can have her."

"You're considering turning into a catnapper?" Mrs. Ramirez asked with a sly smile on her face.

Grace smiled back, then heaved a heavy sigh. She ducked her head and picked at the bun on her burger, rolling pieces of the soft bread between her fingers and squishing it into dough balls before popping them into her mouth. She hadn't thought about it being catnapping. She just said what was on her mind without thinking.

While Mrs. Ramirez and Emily took their turns, Grace nibbled at her corn on the cob. Mr. Ramirez had grilled tonight, and usually his corn cooked on the grill was her favorite, but tonight she barely tasted the yogurt-chipotle sauce Natalie had drizzled over her ear. And the paprika and cilantro sprinkled on it seemed almost flavorless. All she could think about was saying good-bye to Chances, which would be horrible. But even worse would be knowing she was heading to one of those owners.

"Abby, can I ask you something?" Grace said.

Every head swiveled toward Grace. Mr. Ramirez's forehead wrinkled in confusion. "Grace, Natalie was right in the middle of her story. She listened politely to your story, so I expect you to be equally as mannerly and listen to hers."

Grace squirmed in her chair. She had no idea she'd interrupted her sister. This time she forced herself to pay attention, but in the back of her mind, she was busy devising schemes to save Chances. As soon as Natalie finished, Grace repeated her question to Abby.

"Abby, how do you pick the best owners for your puppies?" Grace asked.

Grace listened carefully to Abby's advice. "But what if none of the owners are the right ones?"

"Then I wouldn't let anyone have them," Abby replied matter-of-factly.

Grace sighed. That wasn't an option here, but she couldn't think of any other solutions.

The next morning she trudged to Miz Ida's, gripping her notebook, still uncertain which person to recommend.

Miz Ida greeted her at the door. "A mother called me early this morning to beg me to sell the cat to her. She promised her three children would love it. She'd almost convinced me until she mentioned their other two cats had disappeared."

"I'm glad you didn't choose her," Grace said. "I'd hate to think of Chances disappearing."

"I agree," Miz Ida said. "So what notes did you take yesterday?"

Grace flipped open her notebook and read what she'd written. "Oops, I guess I forgot to write down positive things about each person." She'd been so focused on why the people they'd interviewed would be wrong for Chances.

"Some positives would help," Miz Ida said. "Let's see. The first lady was willing to pay full price, and Chances would be featured in a magazine. The second knew a lot about pedigrees, and the third seemed to be an expert in breeding. I'm sure they'd all take good care of her."

Grace pinched her lips together so she didn't say those three would only take care of Chances for their own benefit, not because they loved her. They were supposed to be concentrating on positives right now. She couldn't think of any positives to add, so she stayed quiet.

Miz Ida stood. "Thank you for all your input, Grace. Making this decision isn't easy, and I wish I didn't have to do it so quickly. But Roger will arrive in two days to help me pack. Before that, I want Chances to go to the best home possible."

"I do too," Grace burst out. She was positive none of those homes would be right for Chances. "Have you decided on any of them yet?" She wasn't sure she wanted to hear the decision.

"I believe I have." But when Grace asked who she'd chosen, Miz Ida said, "Why don't you help me get her ready to go to her new home first? Then I'll tell you my decision."

Grace trailed Miz Ida into the trophy room. Chances lay curled in the sunshine on one of her scratching-post platforms, but when they entered, she stretched and meowed. She headed straight for Grace, rubbed against her legs, and purred. Blinking back tears, Grace bent and scratched Chances behind the ears. The Persian turned her head and ran her rough pink tongue over Grace's hand.

"I'll miss you, Chances," Grace whispered, her throat tight. She hoped Miz Ida would let her brush the cat today and tomorrow before Chances was gone for good.

Chances stayed beside Grace, pouncing on her shoelaces or batting her ankles, while she helped Miz Ida carefully pack all the ribbons and trophies into plastic storage bins. As the walls grew barer, Grace's heart grew heavier, and she could barely hold back

her tears. She couldn't imagine these awards hanging on the walls of any of the potential owners' houses. Then they packed up all Chances's toys except her favorite catnip mouse. Finally, Miz Ida asked Grace to groom Chances.

As Grace slid the comb and then the brush through Chances's silky fur, she couldn't hold her tears back anymore. They fell softly like the white fur as it settled on the mat.

"Oh, Grace, I didn't mean to make you cry." Miz Ida looked distraught. "I only wanted my decision to be a surprise." She put a hand on Grace's shoulder.

"After considering all my options, I decided the best owner for Chances is *you*."

"Me? You're giving me Chances?" The brush in Grace's hands went flying, and Chances yowled and raced off. Grace leapt up from the floor to do a happy dance.

"I can't believe it!" She hugged herself, imagining Chances sleeping next to her on the bed at night. She pictured herself brushing the cat's fur, cuddling her, and hearing her purr. It would ease her loneliness, especially at night.

"If you'd like to have her." Miz Ida's eyes twinkled.

"Yes, yes, yes! Oh, yes!!" Grace jumped up and down. She had no idea where they'd put all the ribbons and trophies, but that was only a small problem compared to the joy of having Chances. A pet of her own. A real championship cat.

Then all the excitement leaked out of Grace, leaving her as deflated as a popped balloon. Thinking before acting ruined so many exciting moments. "I guess I should think before I say yes," she said.

One by one, she mentally listed the reasons why she couldn't or shouldn't have a cat. She hadn't asked her parents, she didn't know anything about showing cats, and she didn't know if Emily would like sharing their room with a cat. But the biggest reason of all was that she couldn't afford to pay the price Miz Ida was asking. She should have thought of that before saying "yes."

Grace hung her head. "I'm sorry, Miz Ida, but I can't take Chances."

Miz Ida looked disappointed. "You don't want her?"

"I want her more than anything," Grace admitted. "But after thinking about it, I realize I shouldn't have agreed."

"I know she's a lot of work, but I was hoping you'd take her. It would ease my mind knowing she's in a good home." Miz Ida studied Grace's face. "Would you be willing to share your reasons?"

"I wouldn't mind the work, Miz Ida, but—" Grace proceeded to list her reasons. She gulped when she got to the final one. "And probably most important, I don't have enough money to pay for her."

"Oh, Grace, I didn't intend to charge you anything. I'd just be happy to have Chances in a loving home," Miz Ida said.

Grace blinked. Had she heard that right? Miz Ida wanted to give her Chances?

Miz Ida smiled. "All the other reasons you listed are good ones, though. Tell you what, why don't you go home and check with your family tonight? Then you can let me know tomorrow."

"Thank you. I will." Grace floated out Miz Ida's door and skipped down her long driveway. She remembered to stop and look both ways before crossing the street.

Early the following morning, Grace knocked on Miz Ida's door, her face aching from smiling so much.

"Let me guess," Miz Ida said. "The answer is *yes*."

"Yes, yes, and yes!" She danced inside to help Miz Ida coax Chances into the cat carrier. Then, loaded down with food, bowls, and the catnip mouse, Grace headed home. Mr. Ramirez would stop by that evening to pick up the rest of Chances's things, including all the awards. He even planned to turn a wall in the family room into a spot to display Chances's awards. It wasn't as big as the room at Miz Ida's, but Grace would put the scratching-post tree in the corner of her bedroom near a sunny window so Chances could curl up there and feel at home.

Grace paid extra-careful attention crossing the road because now she had a cat to care for. A cat of her very own. A cat that now belonged to her because she had taken chances. A cat who belonged on Second Chance Ranch because Grace had rescued Chances not once, but twice.

About the Author

When she was young, Laurie J. Edwards brought home many stray dogs and cats. She told her mother they just followed her home, but pieces of leftover meat from her lunch also might have helped to attract them. The pet she wanted most, though, was a horse. Her parents insisted their yard was too small. When she turned thirteen, Laurie began taking riding lessons and spent as much time as she could around horses.

She grew up and became a librarian because she loved books as much as she loved animals. Then she discovered the joys of writing books as well as reading them. Now she is the author of more than 40 books.

About the Illustrator

Jomike Tejido is an author and illustrator who has illustrated the books *I Funny: School of Laughs* and *Middle School: Dog's Best Friend*, as well as the Pet Charms and I Want to Be . . . Dinosaurs! series. He has fond memories of horseback riding as a kid and has always liked drawing fluffy animals. Jomike lives in Manila with his wife, his daughter Sophia, and a chow chow named Oso.

Join Natalie, Abby, Emily, and Grace and
read more animal stories in . . .

BY KELSEY ABRAMS

ILLUSTRATED BY JOMIKE TEJIDO

CHARMING MIDDLE GRADE FICTION
FROM JOLLY FISH PRESS